UNSEEN, UNHEARED, UNSTOPPABLE

CHAPTER-1 : A GIRL IS BORN

The clock on the hospital wall struck 7:14 PM when the sound of a newborn's cry pierced through the corridor. It was sharp, strong, and steady — like she had already sensed the fight waiting for her outside the womb.

The nurse, dressed in a pale blue uniform and holding a clipboard under her arm, stepped out of the labor room and looked around.

The corridor was filled with family members. Her father stood with arms crossed, pacing. The grandmother sat on the metal bench, murmuring silent prayers under her breath. An uncle checked his phone, while an aunt leaned against the wall, already whispering predictions about the child.

The nurse's face was unreadable. "It's a girl," she announced flatly.

For a moment, no one reacted.

Then came the sound of a long sigh. The grandmother closed her eyes and shook her head. "God gives daughters to test us," she said quietly.

The father turned his face away, pretending to read a health poster on the wall. The uncle scratched his head. The aunt gave a weak smile and said, "Well... healthy baby, at least?"

Not one word of joy. Not one clap, not one cheer. No one asked to see her.

Inside the room, the mother lay weak and trembling. Sweat clung to her forehead and neck. Her body ached in places she hadn't known could ache. But when they placed the tiny bundle in her arms, all the pain melted away in a heartbeat.

The baby was small, with a head full of dark hair and the softest pink skin. Her eyes blinked slowly under the dim hospital light,

adjusting to this harsh world she had just entered.

"She's beautiful," the mother whispered.

The nurse smiled gently. "She's strong too. Loud lungs. That's a good sign."

The mother kissed her daughter's forehead. Her hands were shaking, not from weakness, but from the weight of what she already knew. In her heart, she had hoped — prayed — that this child would be a boy. Not because she wanted one more than a daughter, but because she knew what it meant to be a girl in this house.

Her own life had been a story of compromise and silence. Of giving up dreams before they could even form fully. Of swallowing opinions. Of shrinking. She had married young, stayed quiet, and lived in the shadows of others.

Now, this little one — this tiny flame in her arms — was born into the same cage. But maybe, just maybe, she could be the one to break it.

They named her *Aarohi* — the name the mother had silently saved for years. It meant "ascending melody," a name chosen in secret, away from her in-laws' judgment. When the grandmother insisted they name her after an elder relative, the mother nodded and agreed in front of everyone — but at night, she whispered to her baby, "You are my Aarohi. And you always will be."

Back at home, there were no celebrations. No balloons or garlands hung at the entrance. When Aarohi's brother had been born three years ago, the house

had turned into a festival ground. Loud music played till midnight. Neighbors came with gifts. Plates of sweets were handed out like it was Diwali. Her father had taken the entire week off work to "be with his son."

This time, no sweets were ordered. The grandmother muttered something about "bad timing" and "past karma." The father left for work the very next morning.

The neighbors didn't bother to visit.

Inside the house, Aarohi slept in a wooden crib pushed against the corner of the bedroom. Her cries

were met with annoyance. Her diapers changed with a frown. Her mother did everything — fed her, bathed her, sang lullabies when no one was around — but never too loudly, never too happily. She wasn't allowed to show too much affection, as if love for a daughter was some sort of weakness.

Still, Aarohi grew — slowly, silently, and watchfully.

Her eyes were sharp. Always moving. She watched her mother's movements like a shadow. She smiled when she saw her brother's toys but was never allowed to touch them. She cried loudly when left alone, but no one picked her up except her mother.

One day, when she was barely six months old, her grandmother looked at her and said, "You'll be just like your mother — quiet and obedient. That's all a girl needs to be."

The mother overheard this, and for the first time in years, something stirred inside her. A mix of anger and sadness. She walked into the room, lifted Aarohi in her arms, and whispered firmly into her tiny ears:

"You don't have to be quiet, my girl. You don't have to shrink. One day, you will rise so high they'll be forced to look up to you."

Aarohi's little hand reached up and clutched her mother's finger tightly — as if making a silent promise in return.

That night, as the world slept, the mother sat beside the window, rocking her baby to sleep.

Outside, the moon was full — calm, glowing, and untouched by the opinions of others.

Inside, Aarohi breathed softly in her arms.

The mother looked at her
and thought, Maybe the
world didn't celebrate your
birth... but one day, they'll
remember it.

Chapter 2: The Unwanted Celebration

The scent of ghee, sugar, and cardamom floated through the house. Balloons bobbed against the ceiling, and a paper banner that read *"Happy Birthday, Ayush!"* hung crookedly across the wall. Loud music played in the background as guests laughed and plates clinked in the kitchen. The house buzzed with energy — Ayush was turning six today. Aarohi, just three years old, sat quietly in a corner wearing an old frock that used to belong to her cousin. Her hair was tied into two small ponytails, a bit uneven, and she held a small balloon in her hand — the only one she was allowed to take from the decoration box.

She watched her brother zoom past her, wearing a brand-new T-shirt with cartoon characters and shiny shoes. He was busy showing off his toy robot to his friends. Every few minutes, someone would hand him a gift, kiss his cheek, or tell him how smart and handsome he looked.

No one looked at Aarohi.

Not even once.

She wandered into the kitchen, where her mother was sweating over a stove, frying hot samosas. "Mumma," she whispered, tugging her dupatta, "can I get a chocolate too?"

Her mother glanced around to make sure no one was watching, then quickly slid one piece into her tiny hand. "Shh... eat it here only, okay? Don't let Dadi see."

Aarohi didn't understand why her joys had to be hidden — but she was too young to question. She smiled and took small bites, savoring each one.

Two months later, on Aarohi's fourth birthday, the house was unusually quiet.

There were no balloons. No decorations. No guests.

Just the regular chaos of a typical morning — her grandmother yelling at the maid, her father reading the newspaper, and Ayush complaining about his school shoes.

Aarohi sat at the edge of the bed, wearing her favourite yellow frock — the one with small sunflowers that her mother had saved for special occasions. She had woken up early, excitement fluttering in her chest. She thought maybe there'd be a cake... or a surprise gift... or at least a

"Happy Birthday" from someone.

Instead, what she got was a half-hearted "Hmm... birthday today?" from her father and a reminder from her grandmother: "Don't expect anything just because you were born. Girls should be grateful they're fed." Her small face fell. Her eyes didn't tear up, but her lips quivered. She tried to stay cheerful — she didn't want her birthday to be ruined, even if no one cared.

Her mother brought her a bowl of kheer in the afternoon — just one bowl, made secretly with leftover milk and sugar. She sat beside Aarohi and whispered, "Happy birthday, my jaan. I'm sorry I couldn't do more."

Aarohi gave a tiny smile and asked softly, "Why is Ayush bhaiya's birthday so big and mine so small?"

The question hung in the air like a sharp silence.

Her mother looked away, her throat tightening. "Because…

some people think boys are more important than girls."

"But why?" Aarohi asked again.

The mother couldn't answer.

Instead, she hugged her daughter tightly and whispered, "You are more than enough. You're my celebration every single day."

Later that evening, Aarohi sat by the window, holding a tiny piece of newspaper she had folded into the shape of a gift box. Inside, she had hidden a pebble — smooth and shiny — the only "present" she had found in the garden.

She pretended it was a diamond.

She held it close, imagining it was a gift from the world — proof that even if no one celebrated her, the sky, the wind, and the stars did.

She looked up and said to herself, "One day, the whole world will celebrate my birthday. There will be lights... and music... and even Dadi will clap."

And then she smiled.

Not because she believed it fully yet — but because something inside her refused to stop dreaming.

Chapter 3: Shadows of a Brother's Glory

"Bhaiya got first prize again!" the grandmother announced loudly as she waved the certificate in the air like a victory flag. "Just look at him— topper of his class, just like his father!"

Ayush stood in the center of the living room, holding his golden trophy with a proud smirk on his face. His school tie was still on, swinging side to side as he soaked in the applause. The room echoed with praise — uncles clapped, aunts gushed, and the neighbours nodded in approval.

Aarohi, now six, stood at the doorway with her schoolbag still on her shoulders. Dust clung to her socks, and her notebook peeked out from the half-open zip. No one noticed that she was home. No one asked how her day was. No one even saw the *"Well Done!"* sticker on the front page of her English notebook.

She walked to the corner, quietly took off her shoes, and sat near the window, pulling out the sticker and running her finger over it. Her teacher had written in red ink:

"Beautiful handwriting, Aarohi! Very neat!"

She smiled to herself for a second.

Then she heard her grandmother's voice again — sharp, proud, and echoing

through the house:
"See! This is why boys are a blessing! Look at his achievements — medals, trophies, always number one! And what does the girl do? Always quiet, always in her books, but no spark!"

Aarohi flinched. She hadn't expected her to say it so directly, not today — not when she had also tried her best. But she said nothing.

She had learned early: if you speak, they say you're arguing. If you stay silent, they say you're dull. There was no winning.

The next week, the school held a storytelling competition.

Aarohi had prepared for days. She stayed up late, sitting with her mother and practicing each word. Her story was simple but full of heart — about a little sparrow who wanted to fly higher than the eagles. Her mother clapped softly every time she finished.

"You'll win," she said, kissing Aarohi's forehead. "Just be yourself."

And she did win.

First prize. A shining silver medal. The school principal even called her "brilliant with imagination." Aarohi came home with stars in her eyes, gripping her medal tightly. She couldn't wait to show everyone.

But when she entered, the house was chaotic again — Ayush had just returned from cricket trials and had been selected for the district team.

There were sweets on the table, loud conversations, and phone calls going out to every relative.

She stood near the sofa, medal in hand, waiting.

Waiting to be seen.

Waiting for someone to ask why she was smiling so wide.

But no one did.

Eventually, she walked up to her father and quietly said, "Papa... I also won something today."

He turned briefly, distracted. "Hmm? What was it?"

"A medal... for storytelling."

"Oh," he said, nodding. "Good. But did Ayush tell you? He got selected! That's a big deal, okay? Cricket is no joke."

He turned back to the conversation. Aarohi's hands dropped to her sides. The medal suddenly felt heavier.

She went to her room, opened the old steel cupboard, and kept the medal inside a plastic box that already held a few drawings, a certificate from her dance performance, and a poem she had written but never shared. Her mother had once told her to keep all her 'achievements' there.

"I'll build you a shelf one day," her mother had said. "A place to display all this."

But the shelf never came. There was always an excuse. Always another priority.

Always Ayush.

That night, lying in bed beside her mother, Aarohi finally asked the question that had been burning in her chest for months.

"Mumma… am I invisible?"

Her mother's eyes widened. "What? No, beta. Why would you say that?"

"Because when Ayush bhaiya wins, everyone claps. And when I do something good… it's like it doesn't matter."

The mother swallowed hard. She had no words — because deep down, she had asked herself the same thing for years.

She hugged Aarohi close. "You are not invisible. You are just... shining in a place where people refuse to look."

"But what's the use of shining if no one sees it?"

Her mother was quiet.

Then, after a long pause, she whispered, "Sometimes, the brightest stars are the ones you can't see during the day... but when the night comes — when it gets really dark — they're the only light left in the sky."

Aarohi didn't fully understand the metaphor. But she held on to the words.

She decided, silently, that one day she would become so bright... that even the people who refused to look at her would be blinded by her light.

Chapter 4: A Dream is Planted

The school fair was Aarohi's favourite day of the year.

Stalls lined the dusty playground — bursting with colourful crafts, snacks, games, and laughter. Students were allowed to run small businesses for a day, with money collected for charity. It was the only time Aarohi felt like school was more than just rules and timetables. It felt... free.

This year, her class had to come up with ideas for their own stall. While most of the children suggested games or food, Aarohi raised her hand slowly.

"What if we make handmade bookmarks with positive quotes?" she said, eyes lighting up. "We can paint them ourselves and add ribbons! They'll be easy to make and people can gift them too."

For a moment, there was silence. Then the teacher

smiled and said, "That's a brilliant idea, Aarohi."

The whole class agreed. The next week was full of colour. Aarohi stayed after school, helping her friends make dozens of bookmarks. She brought glitter from home. She wrote tiny quotes on each one — things like *"You Matter"*, *"Dream Big"*, and *"Keep Growing."*

The day of the fair arrived. Their stall was simple — just a wooden table with a chart that said *"Kind Words Corner"* — but it was the most popular one in the row. Teachers stopped by. Even parents from other classes came to buy bookmarks. Some bought two, some bought five. A few came back asking if there were more.

By the end of the day, they had sold *everything*.

"We earned 580 rupees!" the teacher beamed. "That's more than double any other stall!"

The whole group cheered. Aarohi felt something bloom in her chest — not just happiness, but a spark. A feeling she hadn't felt before.

That night, while sitting with her mother, she said softly, "Mumma... I think I want to start a business when I grow up."

Her mother looked at her in surprise. "Business? Like what?"

"Anything," Aarohi said, her eyes dreamy. "I want to sell things that make people smile. Maybe a shop. Or a company. Or something online. But something that's mine. Something that starts from my own hands."

Her mother paused, brushing Aarohi's hair back gently.

"Not many girls in this family think like that," she said. "But you... you've always been different."

Aarohi smiled and looked up at the ceiling, imagining it — her own office, her own brand, her own name on something big.

But her dream wasn't met with applause the next day.

At dinner, when she proudly said, "I want to be a businesswoman," her grandmother scoffed.

"Business? Girls don't run businesses. They run homes."

Her father looked up from his phone. "You're too young to say things like that."

Ayush laughed. "You? A businesswoman? With what money?"

Aarohi shrank in her seat. Her cheeks burned, but her voice stayed calm.

"I'll find a way," she said, softly but surely.

No one listened.

But she knew, deep in her heart, something had been planted that day.

Not just a wish. Not just a passing thought.

A dream.

Chapter 5: Rules Written for Boys

Aarohi was ten the first time she was told she *couldn't* do something just because she was a girl.

Not because it was dangerous.
Not because she was too young.
But simply... because *she wasn't a boy.*

It started small.

Ayush was allowed to ride his bicycle outside the colony

gate. Aarohi had to stay inside.

Ayush could go to the tuition class alone. Aarohi had to wait for the maid to take her.

Ayush went to cricket matches with friends on Sundays. Aarohi stayed home to "help her mother learn responsibility."

It never made sense.

She once asked, "Why can't I go out with my friends too?"

Her father replied without even looking up, "Because girls need to be protected."

Aarohi frowned. "But who will protect me when I grow up?"

Her grandmother cut in sharply: "You'll have a husband for that."

The room fell silent. Aarohi didn't respond. But something inside her felt like it had snapped.

One day, while flipping through an old magazine her mother had brought from a friend's house, Aarohi saw a photo that stopped her in her tracks.

It was a giant hotel lobby — with sparkling chandeliers, velvet sofas, and a woman in a navy-blue suit standing confidently at the front desk. The caption read:

"Meera Khanna: India's Youngest Luxury Hotel Owner"

Aarohi stared at the image for minutes.

She wasn't sure what she felt.

Excitement?

Admiration?

Jealousy?

No... it was something bigger. Something brighter. Something *pulling* her forward.

She ran to her mother and asked, "Can I keep this page?"

Her mother glanced at it. "Why?"

"Because I want to be like her. I want to open a hotel too... a big one. With beautiful rooms and food from all over the world. People will come to stay and feel

happy. And I'll treat them like family."

Her mother smiled softly. "That's a big dream, beta."

"I know," Aarohi whispered. "But it's mine."

She kept the page folded inside her diary. Every few nights, she would take it out, stare at it again, and imagine what her hotel would look like.

She even gave it a name:

"Aaranya — A Place to Belong"

She scribbled down ideas — room designs, menu items, welcome gifts for guests, even uniforms for

staff. Her notebook slowly turned into a blueprint of her dream.

But while her imagination soared, reality kept pulling her down.

One evening, as Ayush and his friends played cricket in the alley, Aarohi sat by the window, sketching hotel room layouts on the back of her math homework.

Her grandmother walked in, saw the page, and scoffed.

"What is this nonsense? You should be learning how to make rotis. Not building castles in the air."

Aarohi didn't respond.

"Mark my words," Dadi said, her voice sharp. "This dreaming will ruin your marriage. No good family wants a girl who thinks she's equal to men."

She left the room muttering, leaving behind a chill of anger and humiliation.

But Aarohi didn't tear the page.

She folded it carefully, placed it inside her box of dreams, and wrote underneath it in bold letters:

"I am not a castle in the air. I am the builder of it."

That night, lying in bed, she whispered to herself, "One hotel isn't enough. I want many. I want a chain — in every city, every state. Places where people feel safe. Especially girls.

Especially the ones who are told they *can't*."

It wasn't just a dream anymore.

It was a mission.

Aarohi didn't have support. She didn't have money. She didn't even have permission.

But she had vision.

And sometimes, that's the
only thing you need to begin.

Chapter 6: The Mirror of Expectations

Middle school came with new books, taller benches, and an invisible rulebook that no one ever handed to Aarohi — but somehow, everyone expected her to follow.

Her life began to split in two.

In school, she was known as the *"smart girl"* — teachers praised her discipline, her handwriting, her respectful tone. She helped organize events, won elocution contests, and was often picked as the group leader. Her friends

admired her. Some even said, "You're like a role model."

But at home, she was something else entirely —
the girl who must not cross lines.

She was expected to:

- come straight home from school,
- help in the kitchen,
- not raise her voice,

- never question elders,
- and most importantly — **not dream beyond marriage.**

Ayush, on the other hand, was becoming louder, bolder, and more careless by the day. He left his shoes in the living room,

shouted during online games, skipped homework — but still got praised for being "young and energetic."

Aarohi, even when quiet and composed, was often told, "Don't act too smart."

"Girls with attitude don't get good husbands."
"Control your tone."

It felt like there was a giant mirror in her house — one she was constantly being asked to stand in front of — to check if she looked like the kind of girl society approved of.

Neat.
Polite.
Small.
Silent.

She once overheard a conversation between her aunt and her grandmother in the kitchen:

"She's too ambitious. That girl Aarohi. Always lost in books and ideas."

"She needs to be reminded she's a girl. Her wedding, not a career, is her future."

The words stung. Not because they were surprising — but because they weren't.

One Sunday afternoon, Aarohi sat with her mother, peeling peas for lunch. It was one of the few quiet, warm moments they shared when no one else was around.

"Mumma," she asked softly, "did you ever want to do something... big?"

Her mother paused, looked down at her hands, and smiled — but there was sadness in it.

"I wanted to be a teacher," she said. "Even applied for a training course once. But your Dadi said it wasn't needed. Said girls don't need jobs when they'll have husbands to feed them."

Aarohi stared. "So you just… stopped?"

Her mother nodded. "Sometimes, stopping isn't a choice. It's made for you."

Aarohi said nothing. But her hands began to peel the peas faster. Her heart, however, started peeling the layers of every "no" she had ever been given.

And suddenly, she wasn't afraid anymore — she was angry.

Not the loud, explosive kind.

But the kind that simmers quietly in the soul... and fuels revolutions.

That evening, she looked into the mirror in her room.

She adjusted her dupatta like Dadi always told her to.

She lowered her eyes like Papa said "good girls" should.

She smiled softly the way her aunt said "men liked."

And then... she looked herself straight in the eye and whispered,

"I will never be what they expect. I will be what I choose."

She wrote those words on the first page of her new diary.

And underneath it, she drew a hotel — tall, proud, with her name on top.

Chapter 7: *A Letter to Her Future*

It was raining outside — one of those gentle, poetic rains that made the world feel softer, sadder, and somehow more honest.

Aarohi sat by the window, hugging her knees, watching the drops slide down the glass. Everyone else was busy — Ayush playing video games, Papa scrolling through news, Dadi complaining about the electricity bill, and

Mummy cooking quietly, as always.

She felt invisible again.

Like her presence was only noticed when she made a mistake.
Like she was only remembered when there was work to be done.
Like being a daughter... was a role, not a person.

She reached for her diary, flipped to a fresh page, and wrote in bold:

***To the Aarohi who made it
to the future,***

For a second, she froze.
She had never written a
letter to herself before.
But somehow, this one didn't
feel silly.
It felt necessary.

So she kept writing.

"I don't know where you are right now. Maybe you're in a small room, struggling to build your first hotel. Maybe you're still stuck in a house where no one believes in you. Or maybe... you've already built something

beautiful, and this letter is just a reminder of where it all started.

Today, I feel small. Not because I am — but because everyone around me wants me to be.

They tell me:
'Be quiet. Be good. Be

simple. Be like other girls.'
But I don't want to be like
other girls.
I want to be like *me*.

I want to wake up in a hotel
room designed by me, with
staff who feel like family. I
want to welcome guests
with warm food, clean beds,
fresh flowers, and smiles
that heal. I want my hotel

to feel like home for people
who've never had one.

I want to give jobs to
women who were told they
couldn't work.
I want to build a place

where no one asks, 'But
you're just a girl, right?'
I want to prove that being a
girl is not a weakness.
It's the beginning of
strength.

I hope you've held on.
I hope you didn't let their
voices drown yours.
And even if you're still
fighting — that's okay.
Because every fight you pick
for yourself is worth it."

She stopped, tears in her eyes.

Not from sadness — but from the feeling of *finally* being heard… even if it was by herself.

She signed it:
— Aarohi (age 13, but dreaming bigger than the world)

She folded the letter, placed it inside her diary, and whispered,
"I'll read this again when I make it."

She didn't know how.
She didn't know when.
But she believed.

And sometimes, belief is the first brick in building an empire.

Chapter 8: *When Silence Starts Screaming*

Aarohi had mastered the art of silence.

She knew when to nod. When to lower her eyes. When to smile politely — even when her heart wanted to scream.

But silence isn't always peace. Sometimes, it's a storm waiting for the right gust of wind to break loose.

At the dinner table one night, Papa was praising Ayush for helping him at the shop for an hour.

"See how responsible he's becoming," he said, proudly patting Ayush's back. "He'll handle the business one day."

Aarohi looked up. "I can help too... if you want."

The room went quiet. Her father looked at her, confused.

"You? Help at the shop? Why?"

"Just to learn," she replied, steady. "I like learning how things work."

Dadi didn't wait even a second.

"Girls don't sit behind counters. They sit in the kitchen," she snapped.

Mummy looked at Aarohi with soft warning eyes — *not now*, they seemed to say. Ayush smirked. Papa changed the topic.

But something had changed inside Aarohi.

Something that couldn't be silenced anymore.

Over the next few weeks, the moments stacked up:

- When she got the highest marks in class, but her father only asked, "Did Ayush do well too?"

- When her cousin was allowed to go for an out-of-town workshop, but she was told, "It's not safe for girls."

- When she designed a mini hotel model for a school project and her uncle laughed, "Building hotels, haan? First learn how to make tea!"

It wasn't about the words anymore.

It was the weight of them.

The way they dismissed her without even thinking.
The way her dreams were treated like jokes.

The way her silence was taken as agreement.

One night, unable to sleep, Aarohi stepped onto the balcony. The air was cool, but her chest felt heavy.

She stared at the stars, her fists clenched around the railing.

She didn't cry.

She didn't shout.

But inside her, something was screaming. Loudly.

**"Why is everything I love...
wrong?"**
**"Why do I have to shrink to
fit their comfort?"**
**"Why do I need permission
to be *me*?"**

And then, quietly...
Aarohi answered herself:
"I don't."

Not anymore.

That night, she opened her
diary again — and started
writing her hotel plan, in full
detail this time.
Not for a school project.
Not for approval.

But for her.

She started researching names of hotel owners. She drew logo ideas. She listed themes — from eco-hotels to heritage ones. She even made a mini map of where her first hotel could be: maybe in the mountains, or near a beach.

Her room became her secret universe.

Where her voice was loud. Where she was respected. Where dreams weren't laughed at — they were built.

People say silence is golden.

But for girls like Aarohi?

Silence becomes a scream.
And screams become
blueprints.

And blueprints become
revolutions.

Chapter 9: *The Engagement Everyone Expected*

It started with a tray of tea.

Not in her hands — but in her mind.

Because that's how it always begins in families like hers.

One day you're studying for a test.
The next, you're being told to wear something "nice"

because *"they're coming to see you."*

Aarohi was seventeen when she first heard her name being paired with someone else's in hushed tones.

"He's a nice boy," her aunt whispered to her mother. "Family is decent. Educated. Well-settled."
"And best part," Dadi added, "he doesn't mind if the girl isn't working."

That last sentence made Aarohi stop mid-step in the hallway.

He doesn't mind if the girl isn't working.

Like it was a favour.

Like it was some kind of mercy that the boy would "tolerate" a wife who stayed home — silent, pretty, and dreamless.

Aarohi wasn't even asked.

No one asked if she liked him.
No one asked if she wanted marriage.

No one asked if she had dreams that had nothing to do with kitchens or sarees or bearing children.

At dinner that night, Papa cleared his throat.

"We've started looking. You're at the right age, Aarohi."

She put her spoon down. "The right age... for what?"

"For marriage," he said. "Don't act smart."

"I didn't say I want to get married," she replied.

Dadi snapped, "Girls don't *want*. They accept what's good for them."

Aarohi looked at her mother. Silent. Avoiding her eyes.

She felt like she was falling into a box someone else had folded and sealed.

"But what about my studies? My dream?" she asked quietly.

Ayush laughed, "Hotel dream? You really think people will let a bahu run around managing hotels?

First learn to make a proper chai."

Everyone chuckled.

Except Aarohi.

That night, she stayed awake long after the lights went off.

She stared at the ceiling, heart pounding, thoughts running like trains.

"Is this it?"
"Will I be another woman who folds her dreams like laundry and tucks them away?"
"Will I smile in photos with a

**man I didn't choose,
wearing a saree I didn't pick,
beginning a life I didn't
want?"**

No.

She wouldn't.

A few days later, Aarohi was
called to serve tea to the
family who had come to "see
her."

She stood there, dressed in a
suit she didn't choose, hair
done the way Dadi liked,
eyes low, carrying a tray with
shivering hands.

The boy smiled. Looked "decent." Polite.

But when asked about her dreams, she quietly said, **"I want to build a hotel chain."**

Everyone laughed nervously. Thought she was joking.

But her eyes didn't flinch.

After they left, Papa scolded her.

"Can't you just behave like a normal girl?"

"I am behaving like me," she replied.

And walked away.

For the first time, no one followed.

Chapter 10: *Her Secret Blueprint*

The rishta talks faded.

Maybe because of what she said.
Maybe because she didn't fit the "ideal bride" checklist.
Maybe because they just didn't understand her fire.

Whatever the reason, Aarohi didn't care.

For the first time, she wasn't scared of being "rejected."
In fact, she welcomed it.
Because it gave her something precious: **time.**

Time to plan.
Time to learn.
Time to dream — and this time, **with direction.**

Her room became more than just a place to sleep.

It became a **headquarters.**

On one wall, she stuck photos of hotels from around the world:

- Cozy mountain lodges

- Royal heritage properties

- Beach resorts with fairy lights and wooden decks

Below that, she scribbled questions:

- What makes a hotel feel like home?

- Why do people remember one hotel and forget another?

- How do you start with nothing — and build something unforgettable?

On the other side of her desk, she stuck sticky notes:

- *Learn basic business terms*

- *YouTube videos on hotel management*

- *Understand startup funding*

- *Find successful women hotel owners in India*

She downloaded PDFs on hospitality, watched interviews of women entrepreneurs, followed hotel Instagram pages to study interiors, and began writing her own list of hotel ideas.

But the best part?

She named it.

Aaranya.
A mix of her name and "Aranya" — a Sanskrit word for *forest, peace, natural retreat.*

Because her dream wasn't just about business.

It was about *creating a space of calm in a world that often felt*

chaotic.
A place where people could breathe, heal, and feel safe — just like she always wanted to.

Aaranya wouldn't be a five-star hotel for the rich.
It would be a *soul-star* hotel — for real people.

She even designed a logo: a leaf in the shape of an "A." Simple. Earthy. Beautiful.

And at the bottom of the page, she wrote:

"One day, this logo will be on signboards, coffee mugs, pillow covers... and hearts."

But her dreams still had to hide.

Every time someone knocked on her door, she'd slide her notebook under the pillow. Every time Dadi asked what she was doing, she'd say "homework." Every time Papa peeked into her phone, she'd switch tabs.

Because in a world that didn't believe in her... her

plans had to be **secret weapons.**

And secretly?

She was winning.

That night, as she looked around her "blueprint wall," she whispered:

"They may not believe in me. But someday, they'll walk into *my* hotel... and know I was right."

And for the first time, her silence didn't hurt.

It felt like **power.**

Chapter 11: *A Ray Named Kunal*

It started with a wedding. Not hers — her cousin's.

The kind of loud, colourful chaos where aunties gossip louder than the DJ, kids run wild in glittery outfits, and someone's always yelling, *"Where's the mehendi cone?!"*

Aarohi was there, in a yellow suit, helping with decorations, serving sweets, managing tantrums — a silent all-rounder, as always.

That's when she saw him.

Leaning casually near the entrance, talking to her cousin-brother, wearing a crisp kurta and a calm expression.

Not flashy. Not loud.
Just... steady.

His name? **Kunal Agarwal.**
Distant family friend.
Recently returned from Bangalore after completing his MBA.

They were introduced casually.

"This is Aarohi," her cousin said. "She's the school topper and the family's quiet rebel."

Aarohi smiled awkwardly. "I prefer the term 'dreamer.'"

Kunal smiled too — and said, **"Dreamers make the best rebels."**

She blinked.

Wait... what?

That was the first time someone understood her without asking for a presentation.

Over the next few days, they crossed paths during wedding madness.

- Fixing fairy lights together

- Sharing plates of chaat

- Watching the bride scream during her haldi

- Stealing moments of peace between the chaos

And each time, Aarohi noticed:

Kunal asked the right questions.
He listened more than he spoke.
He didn't interrupt her when she talked about her hotel idea — he asked her about *her vision*.

"Why hotels?" he once asked.

She replied, "Because the world needs more safe spaces. Especially for women. I want to build something that welcomes, protects, and inspires."

He nodded thoughtfully.

"You know... I think *Aaranya* will be a name people remember."

Her heart skipped.

She hadn't even told him the name yet.

He had seen the sketch on her notebook when she wasn't even looking.

By the time the wedding ended, the whispers had already started.

"Maybe Kunal and Aarohi would be a good match."

"Both educated. Calm.

Balanced."
"He's broad-minded, I've heard."
"He lets girls work."

But for Aarohi, this wasn't about marriage.

It was about **connection.**

And for the first time, she thought:
Maybe if life puts me with someone... let it be someone who doesn't clip my wings.

Let it be someone like **Kunal**.

A few weeks later, her parents told her over dinner:

"The Agarwals have shown interest. They want to talk about your and Kunal's match."

Her fork froze mid-air.

She looked up, heart pounding.

And for once, Dadi didn't scold her.
Papa didn't mock her.

There was... a pause.
Like they were waiting to hear *what she wanted.*

Later that night, she texted Kunal.

Aarohi: "Are you okay with all this rishta talk?"
Kunal: "Only if you are."
Aarohi: "I'm not a regular kind of bahu."
Kunal: "Good. I'm not looking for a regular life."

And just like that — it began.

Not a fairytale.
Not a rescue mission.
But a bond based on **respect, not roles.**

Chapter 12: *Hopes in Hushed Voices*

Aarohi's engagement was a quiet affair — just close family, a few sweets, and a lot of silent judgments hiding behind fake smiles.

Everyone called it a "perfect match."
But Aarohi? She was still observing.

Because love is one thing.
Marriage... is a whole other story.

After the engagement, she was invited to the Agarwals house — "to get to know the family better."

It looked perfect from the outside.

Big house. Big car. Well-spoken people. English words mixed with tradition.
Aarohi thought maybe, *just maybe*, she was finally stepping into a world where her dreams wouldn't be laughed at.

But the first crack came quickly.

During tea, her future mother-in-law, Mrs. Agarwal, smiled and said,

"So beta, now that you're going to be part of our home, we'll teach you some family recipes."

Aarohi nodded politely.

Then she added, "And Kunal told us you're interested in business?

That's nice, but after marriage, you'll have other priorities, hmm?"

Aarohi smiled — but her heart dropped a little.

Later, in the kitchen, one of the aunties whispered, "You're lucky. Kunal is a good boy. He won't *stop* you from working. But don't expect the family to support such things."

Lucky?

For what — *permission to exist as herself?*

That night, she messaged Kunal.

Aarohi: "Your mom thinks I'll stop dreaming after marriage."

Kunal: "She doesn't mean it that way."

Aarohi: "Then what way *does* she mean it?"

Kunal: "Just give it time. Things will adjust."

Aarohi stared at the message.

Adjust.

That word again.

It followed girls like a shadow — from birth to the end.

Adjust in your home.
Adjust in your marriage.
Adjust in your dreams.

She typed, paused, deleted.
Then finally sent:

Aarohi: "I'm not angry. I just want to know... will you stand with me if they don't?"

No reply for 7 minutes.

Then:

Kunal: "I want to. But it's not easy."

That reply stayed with her all night.

It wasn't a "yes."
It wasn't a "no."
It was... fear.

And Aarohi knew something now:

Kunal wasn't the enemy.
But he wasn't a fighter either.

Not yet.

Days passed. Everyone acted like everything was fine.

But Aarohi noticed the signs:

- Every time she brought up her hotel idea, someone changed the topic.

- Every time she mentioned work, the aunties laughed it off: *"After kids maybe."*

- Every time she said "I will," someone else replied "You'll see."

And yet — she kept building. Secretly.

Kept designing Aaranya's interiors.

Kept writing her vision.

Kept watching hotel webinars after midnight.

Because even if the world spoke in hushes...

Her dream was learning to roar.

Chapter 13: *Aaranya or Arranged?*

The wedding planning was in full swing.
And Aarohi?
She was just a guest at her own future.

Every day, there was a new decision to make.

Which color lehenga?
Which designer?
Which date to choose?

Which aunt would bring the ladoos?

Her mother-in-law took charge like a queen.
Her wedding was turning into a grand production.
But no one was asking Aarohi what she wanted — only what they *wanted* her to be.

One day, while picking out jewellery, Aarohi asked her soon-to-be sister-in-law, Ananya,
"Do you think I should pick the gold set or the diamond set?"

Ananya shrugged. "Well, you're going to wear a lot of jewellery now, so... just go with what they tell you."

Aarohi's chest tightened. Was this her future?
To wear gold and diamonds without ever being *asked* what she really wanted?

She pushed the thought aside and focused on the bigger picture.
After all, she was getting married to Kunal. They had shared dreams and plans, right?
Right?

That night, Kunal asked, "Are you excited?"

"I don't know," Aarohi admitted. "Everything feels like it's happening... *around me*. But I don't feel like I'm the one making the decisions."

Kunal frowned, his eyes softening. "I know this isn't easy for you. But we'll figure it out. After marriage, I'll make sure you get time for your business. Just... wait a little longer."

Her stomach sank.
"Wait for what? The rest of my life?"

He sighed. "It's just how things are. You'll see. After marriage, things will settle down, and you'll get your space."

But Aarohi knew deep down:
She was being told to wait for her life to start.
And **waiting** wasn't in her vocabulary anymore.

Aaranya couldn't wait.
Aaranya needed to exist *now*.
She had dreams to chase —
before marriage, not after.
Before the wedding, not after
the ceremony.
Before the "adjustments,"
not after them.

She couldn't just become a
"good wife."
She had already been **Aarohi**
— and that's who she would
stay.

A few days later, Aarohi
found herself in front of her

computer, looking at her hotel blueprint.

Her vision board.
Her designs.
The logo.
Everything.

And just then, she asked herself the hardest question: **"Will I keep building this, or let it go?"**

It wasn't just a hotel.
It was *her identity*.
It was the quiet rebellion that lived inside her.

That night, after the wedding plans had exhausted her, Aarohi sat across from Kunal. She put down her phone.

"Can I talk to you?" she asked, voice steady.

Kunal looked up, surprised. "Of course."

"I've been thinking a lot," Aarohi began. "About the wedding, the traditions, the family. I'm happy

with you. But I'm not sure if I can be happy with everything else."

Kunal didn't say anything at first.

She continued, "I want to have my own career. My own space. And I want to build Aaranya. I don't want to *wait*. I don't want to be the girl in the background while the world makes choices for me."

Kunal was silent for a moment, his face unreadable.
Then, softly, he said, "I can't promise my family will understand. But I'll try. I'll try for you."

Aarohi stared at him, her
heart in her throat.

"Try?" she whispered.
"Try is not enough."

And in that moment, Aarohi
realized something she had
known all along:

No one could save her
dreams but **her**.

She didn't need Kunal's
permission.
She didn't need to wait.
She didn't need to blend in.

She just needed to *be*.

Chapter 14:
Breaking Free, Gently

Aarohi had always been a quiet fighter.

She never yelled.
She never threw tantrums.
She never made a scene.

She made decisions.
And then she **acted**.
Even if it meant walking a lonely road.

That night, she sat with Kunal, her hands shaking but her voice firm.

"I can't keep pretending everything is fine when it's not," she said. "I love you, but I can't be the 'perfect bride' they want me to be. I can't shut down my dreams for anyone. I'm not asking for a 'yes,' I'm asking for *space*."

Kunal's eyes softened, but there was a hint of confusion. "I want to support you, Aarohi. But the pressure from both families... it's going to be difficult."

Aarohi took a deep breath, her voice unwavering. "I know. But I can't live my life in the shadows, waiting for things to change. I need to take control of my future — now, not later."

Kunal was silent for a long moment, the weight of her words sinking in. He nodded slowly, not completely understanding, but respecting her choice.

"I want to try," he said. "I will try to give you that space. But don't expect me to fix everything. I can't do it alone."

"I don't need you to fix everything," Aarohi replied. "I need you to trust me enough to let me try."

The following days weren't easy.
Aarohi had been prepared for the pushback. She had expected the discomfort, the judgment, the silence that came after choosing to speak her truth.

But nothing prepared her for the quiet battle within herself.

She had built *Aaranya*, a vision that could become a reality if she worked hard enough. But the weight of her family's expectations was still heavy on her shoulders. The world was watching her, waiting for her to fail.

She had to carve out her own space, both physically and mentally.

That evening, after a long day of wedding preparations, Aarohi made a decision. She called her parents into her room and closed the door.

"I need to talk to you," she said, her voice steady but her heart racing.

Her parents looked at her, confused.
"About what?" her father asked.

"About the wedding," Aarohi began, choosing her words carefully. "And about my future. I know you're excited about the marriage, but I can't just be a part of this because it's what's expected of me."

Her mother blinked, clearly taken aback. "What do you mean, beta? You don't want this wedding?"

"I want to marry Kunal," Aarohi said softly. "But I can't lose myself in this. I have a future, dreams, things I've been working on for myself. I'm not just a wife-to-be. I'm still Aarohi. I want to build Aaranya. I need you to understand that."

Her mother's face fell, and her father's jaw tightened. They didn't understand. They wouldn't.

But Aarohi held her ground.

"I'm not asking for permission to follow my dreams. I'm telling you that I will."

For the next few weeks, Aarohi continued working on her hotel project, secretly meeting with potential business advisors, watching videos late at night, learning everything she could about hospitality management.

But she didn't just build her dream in silence. She made small but deliberate steps.

She opened a bank account for her business.
She began sketching out plans for her first property.
She found a mentor online who was willing to guide her.

Every day, she grew stronger. And with every decision she made, she felt herself reclaiming a piece of her future.

But the tension in the air was thick.

Her family was starting to feel the shift. Her in-laws, especially, didn't understand why she wasn't "settling down" the way they expected. The snide comments started. The whispers. The subtle remarks about how she was "too ambitious" for a girl.

But Aarohi refused to be swayed.

One evening, after a particularly tense family dinner, she looked around the table and said, "I don't need your approval. I just need you to accept me for who I am. I am not your idea of what a 'perfect' daughter-in-law should be. I will build my future, and I will do it with or without your support."

The room fell silent.

But Aarohi didn't flinch.
Her shoulders were back, her eyes unwavering.

This was it. The moment she had been preparing for.

She didn't need permission to dream.

Chapter 15: *Tides of Change*

Aarohi sat in her room, laptop open, coffee by her side — not just scrolling aimlessly anymore, but researching.

Hotels.
Hospitality.
Startups.
Women entrepreneurs.

Every night she was learning. Every morning she was *building*.

And then one night — it happened.

She stumbled upon an online pitch competition for aspiring women entrepreneurs.
Winner gets ₹5 lakhs in seed funding.
Plus mentorship.
Plus national exposure.

The deadline? Just 5 days away.

Aarohi stared at the screen, her heart pounding.

Could she do this?

Could she pitch *Aaranya* to the world?

The next morning, she didn't hesitate. She registered for the competition.

She stayed up all night building her pitch deck.
Slide by slide.
Word by word.
Dream by dream.

She poured her soul into it — the logo, the mission, the story behind *Aaranya*.

"Aaranya: A space where every woman feels *seen, safe*, and *special*."

When Kunal found out, he was stunned.

"You signed up for a *pitch competition*?!"

Aarohi nodded. "I need this. Even if I don't win, I need to try. For me."

Kunal didn't argue.
He just looked at her — and for the first time, truly *saw* her.

The fire.
The clarity.
The woman he was about to marry.

He smiled softly. "Okay. Let's rehearse it together then."

Aarohi blinked. "You'll help me?"

He nodded. "Of course. You're not alone in this."

For the next few days, they worked in secret.

Practicing the pitch.
Shooting the video.
Refining the numbers.

Kunal used his marketing knowledge to shape her story. Aarohi brought the soul, the vision, the *why*.

They were a team — and this time, not for a wedding.

For a *dream*.

Submission day came.

Aarohi sat with her finger over the "Submit" button.

Kunal squeezed her hand.

She clicked.

Done.

Now... they waited.

One week later. An email.

Subject: "Congratulations — Aaranya makes Top 10 Finalists!"

Aarohi screamed.

Her mother peeked in. "What happened?"

And for the first time ever, Aarohi said with pride:
"I made it. I'm one step closer to building my dream."

Her mother didn't fully understand.

But that didn't matter
anymore.

The finals were virtual.
A panel of judges.
Live questions.
Only *3 minutes* to speak.

When it was Aarohi's turn,
she took a deep breath.

And then — she *spoke*.

Clear. Passionate.
Unapologetic.

She spoke about her journey.
Her hotel vision.
The way women deserve
more

than "adjustments."
The way *Aaranya* would be a
symbol of *freedom*, not just
hospitality.

After she finished, the judges
were quiet.

Then — one of them smiled.

"You speak like someone
who's already built it in her
heart. That's half the battle
won."

Aarohi didn't win the
competition.
She came **second**.

But what she *did* win?
A mentor.
A small investor.
And a feature in a local startup magazine.

Her name. Her face. Her story.
Right there in print.

"Meet Aarohi — The Girl Who Didn't Wait."

The tides had turned.

Aarohi hadn't run away from marriage.
She hadn't disrespected her family.

She had simply... chosen *herself.*

And now?

Now the world was starting to *see* her.

Not as a daughter.
Not as a bride.
But as a **founder**.

Chapter 16:
Between Two Fires

Success felt like sunlight.
Warm. Bright. Blinding.

But sometimes... it also *burned.*

After the pitch competition, Aarohi became a small local sensation.

People started calling her "the girl with the hotel dream."

She got invited to speak at a

college entrepreneurship panel.

A small blog even featured her under **"10 Women to Watch in 2025."**

She was glowing.

But not everyone liked the spotlight on *her*.

At her in-laws' house, the whispers began.

"She's always on her laptop."
"Isn't this wedding distracting her?"
"A hotel? That's no place for a girl to work."

"Bahus should care about the *home*, not business plans."

Her mother-in-law, who had always smiled politely, was now visibly colder.

At dinner, she said casually, "You should focus on settling down first. What will people say if the

bride is chasing businesses instead of learning housework?"

Aarohi smiled politely.

"I'm capable of doing both," she replied.

Her father-in-law put down his spoon. "That's not how it works in our family."

Later that night, Kunal spoke to her privately.
"They're just... old school. It'll take time."

Aarohi turned to him, her voice calm but firm.
"They've had *decades* to evolve.

I've only just *started*. I'm not stepping back now."

Kunal sighed. He supported her — in theory.

But in practice? His silence spoke volumes.

The next few days were tough.
She tried her best to play both roles.

Morning: Meetings with her mentor.
Afternoon: Wedding dress fittings.
Evening: Pre-wedding rituals.
Night: Excel sheets and business plans.

She was juggling dreams and duties — but her hands were shaking.

One afternoon, she was at a family gathering. Her aunt pulled her aside.

"Beta, I heard about your business thing. That's sweet, but you should calm it down now. After marriage, these things don't work."

Aarohi asked, "Why not?"

The aunt smiled. "Because in the end, a woman's real business is her family."

That night, Aarohi cried alone in her room.

Not because of the pressure. But because *she was expected to fold*.

Like her dreams were a phase.
Like *Aaranya* was just a hobby.

She looked at her vision board on her wall — hotel sketches, notes, the words: **"A safe place for women to feel seen."**

And she whispered to herself:

"So why am I letting myself disappear again?"

The next morning, Aarohi made a decision.

She walked into the living room, where her in-laws were having tea.

Calm. Dignified. Unshaken.

"I wanted to inform you — I've been invited to speak at a business conference next week. It's a big opportunity for Aaranya. I will be attending."

Her mother-in-law scoffed. "You didn't ask us."

Aarohi smiled. "I wasn't asking for permission. Just letting you know."

Her father-in-law frowned. "And your wedding preparations?"

"I have managed everything," she said simply. "Like I always do."

After she left the room, the silence behind her was loud.

But so was her heart.

Aarohi knew she was walking between two fires:
The fire of her family's expectations…
And the fire of her *own* becoming.

And guess what?

She was learning how to *dance in the flames*.

Chapter 17: The Stage and the Storm

The hall pulsed with electricity.

Lights. Cameras. Flash. Noise.
Entrepreneurs murmured.
Investors hovered. Phones
buzzed.
But the spotlight found only
one name on everyone's lips.

Aarohi.

Draped in a navy-blue saree
that shimmered like
midnight, she walked like a

storm wrapped in silence. Calm on the outside. But inside? Chaos.

This wasn't just a speech.

It was a reckoning.

And it was hers.

Backstage, she gripped the edge of the vanity. Her bangles rattled against the glass.

This was the biggest moment of her life — and yet, her thoughts kept slipping to her in-laws' cold stares. Her aunt's dismissive smile. The unspoken "no" in Kunal's silence every time she mentioned Aaranya.

Her fingers trembled.

Then—
A touch.

Familiar. Gentle.

Kunal.

He adjusted the mic on her saree. Carefully. Tenderly.

"You look beautiful," he whispered. Then added, more seriously, "And powerful."

Aarohi turned toward the mirror. Their eyes met.
He smiled softly, kissed her forehead.

"Go show them what Aaranya really means."

The stage swallowed her.

The lights went up.

And for a second—she couldn't breathe.

But then... she spoke.

And it all came pouring out.

Not just her business idea.
But *her truth*.

The nights she cried because she was told to shrink.
The days she smiled through people's disbelief.
The ache of dreaming in a world that wanted her to fold.

"The world doesn't need more women who 'adjust,'" she said, voice steady now. "It needs more women who own their dreams — even if it burns."

The room went *still*.

Then—**thunderous applause**.

But she didn't hear it.

Her eyes had already found him.

Kunal.

Front row.

Standing.

But there was something in his gaze.

Not just pride.

Not just love.

Something else.

Finality.

The event ended. Reporters swarmed her.

Flashes. Questions. Praise.

But she wasn't listening.

Because Kunal was already walking toward her — fast, determined.

"Aarohi," he said, his voice quiet but urgent.

She stepped away from the crowd. "What is it? What's wrong?"

He didn't answer.

Instead, he reached into his pocket.

And pulled out...
a key.

She froze.

"Kunal...?"

"I rented a flat last year," he said slowly. "I never used it. I didn't have the courage. But now... I do."

Aarohi stared at it.

"What... what are you saying?"

He took a deep breath. No turning back now.

"I'm saying I'm done watching you fight alone. Done sitting quietly while they try to cut your wings."

He looked at her — eyes burning.

"I love my parents. But I love *you* more. And I'm ready to build something with you. Not beside them. Not beneath their rules. *With you.*"

He held out the key between them.

A choice.

A doorway.

A storm.

Her voice was barely a whisper. "You... you want to move out?"

"I want *us* to live free," he said. "No more whispers. No more permission. Just you, me, and whatever we build next."

Her eyes welled. She looked at the key.

It shimmered in the light — like a weapon. Like a promise.

"You're choosing me?" she asked.

He stepped closer.

"No," he said. "I'm choosing **us**."

Silence.

One heartbeat.
Two.
Three.

Aarohi stared at him — her heart thundering. The world tilted beneath her.
Was this it?

The moment her life finally split in two?

Tears slipped down her cheek.

Her hand moved — slowly — toward the key.

But just before she touched it—

The lights flickered.

A text buzzed on her phone.

A call from her mother.

A knock on the backstage door.

Voices outside. Pressure building.

Her hand hovered.

She looked at Kunal.

Then...

End of Book One.

*Will she say yes?
Or will the fire burn
everything down
first?*

To be continued...